AUG   2001

GOOD MORNING, LITTLE FOX

GOOD MORNING, LITTLE FOX

by MARILYN JANOVITZ

A CHESHIRE STUDIO BOOK

North-South Books · New York · London

Little Fox woke up early.

He climbed into bed with Father Fox.

"It's Saturday," he whispered to his mother. "We're going to sleep late."

"I'll make breakfast," Mother Fox said.

Little Fox and Father Fox curled up close. On the weekend they always did things together.

They heard Mother call. "Breakfast is cooking," she said.

Father Fox stretched and Little Fox yawned.
Slowly they opened their eyes.
Mother Fox called again. "Breakfast is ready," she said.

"And *we're* ready for breakfast," said Father. "Let's eat!"
"Yes," said Little Fox. "Let's eat!"

"I have a surprise," said Mother. "I've made porridge."
"I don't think I like porridge," said Father Fox.
"I don't think I like it either," said Little Fox.
"But you've never tasted it," Mother said. "I tried it and I like it."

"Let's make our own breakfast," said Father.
"We can do that," said Little Fox.

So while Mother ate her porridge, Little Fox and Father Fox looked for something good to eat.

"How about eggs?" said Father. "I like eggs."

"I like eggs too," said Little Fox.

But when they opened the carton, there were no eggs left.
"Well, we can have toast," said Father.
"We like toast," said Little Fox.

But when they looked in the bread box, there was no bread left.
"What about fruit?" said Father. "I like fruit."
"Me too," said Little Fox.

They took down the fruit bowl. It was empty too.

"I'll go to the market," said Mother. "Can you wait to eat till I get back?"

"We can wait," said Little Fox.

"It's the weekend," said Father. "We have things to do."

They folded and they fluffed.

They picked up and they put away.

They even had time to dust.

All that work made them very hungry.

But Mother Fox was still not home, so they went into the kitchen to wait.

There on the table sat the pot of porridge.
Little Fox lifted the lid.
"It smells good," he said.

"It looks good too."

"Maybe we should taste it," said Little Fox.
"If you taste it, I'll taste it," said Father.

And that's just what they did.
They took one taste and then they took another, and then another and then . . .

"Look who's eating my porridge," said Mother Fox.
"We just wanted to taste it," said Little Fox.
Mother Fox smiled. "Let me warm it up," she said.

Mother Fox put the pot of porridge on the stove.

Then she spooned it out and waited for them to finish.

"Well, what do you think?" asked Mother.

"It's not bad," said Father Fox.

"I like it," said Little Fox. "Can I have some more?"

Mother Fox spooned the last of the porridge into his bowl.

And Little Fox ate it all up.

To Suzanne and Truffles

Published in the United States by North-South Books Inc., New York.
Published simultaneously in Great Britain, Canada, Australia, and New Zealand in 2001
by North-South Books, an imprint of Nord-Süd Verlag AG, Gossau Zürich, Switzerland.

Library of Congress Cataloging-in-Publication Data is available.
A CIP catalogue record for this book is available from The British Library.

The illustrations in this book were created
with colored pencil and watercolor.
Designed by Marc Cheshire

ISBN 0-7358-1440-6 (trade binding)
1 3 5 7 9 TB 10 8 6 4 2
ISBN 0-7358-1441-4 (library binding)
1 3 5 7 9 LB 10 8 6 4 2
Printed in Belgium